ZOOMIE & ZOD

AN OPTION-BASED ADVENTURE

*Inter-planetary adventures
in turbulent times for cosmic newlyweds.*

HARLEY KERYLUKE

 FriesenPress

Suite 300 - 990 Fort St
Victoria, BC, V8V 3K2
Canada

www.friesenpress.com

ISBN
978-1-5255-4633-4 (Hardcover)
978-1-5255-4634-1 (Paperback)
978-1-5255-4635-8 (eBook)

1. Young Adult Fiction, Action & Adventure

Distributed to the trade by The Ingram Book Company

TABLE OF CONTENTS

SECTION A

STAR CHART OF UKOPO SOLAR SYSTEM

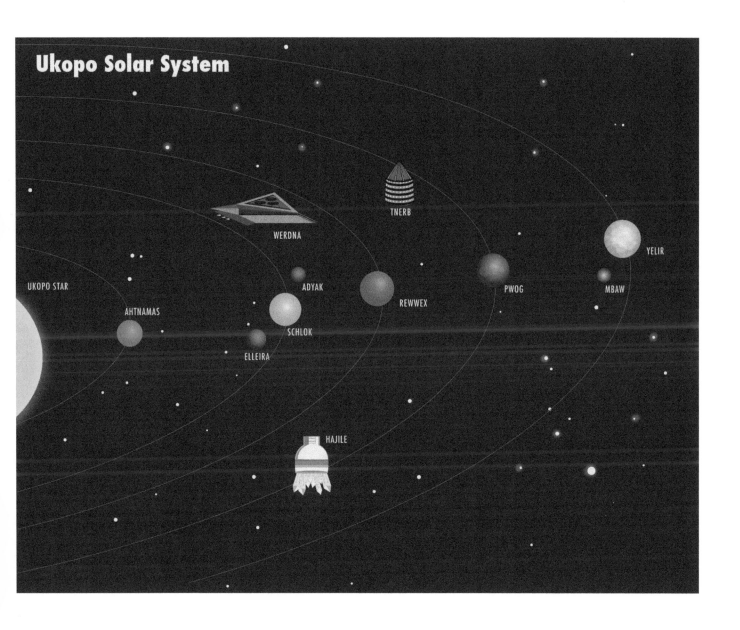

FOREWORD

Ahead of you now are a series of choices directing an option-based adventure. These options are directed by a section letter, an option letter and page number describing the location in the book. These verses describe the setting. You choose the option which directs the actions of our characters.

THE BOOK IS DIVIDED INTO FIVE SECTIONS:

A, B, C, D & E.

You are in the **A** section.

- **A** section contains the Star Chart, Foreword and Points of Interest.

- **B** section is the Introduction to the story.

- **C** section is the beginning content section where the options are available to direct the characters through the adventure.

- **D** section is the content coming to its conclusion with various outcomes available.

- **E** section follows the conclusions with an Appendix.

THE FLAGS:

- The asterisk (*) indicates when to select an A, B, or C option, after the verse is complete.

- There are "flags", such as, **<<Letter. #>>,** that indicate the beginning of a verse, it's option letter and a number for which page the verse is positioned.

EXAMPLE: <<C.27>>

- This example, at the beginning of the verse, denotes that the **C** option, chosen on page **25**, directs us to the verse for option **<<C.27>>,** located on page **27**. At the end of the verse, **<<A.40>>,** is option **A** on page **40,** *or* **<<B.36>>,** is option **B** located on page **36**. This directs us to one of two options. **<<A.40>> or <<B.36>>**

REMINDER:

- Once the options are concluded for the characters, the book may be read again with different options for a new outcome.

- At the back of the book is an Appendix containing a Glossary, in both English and Alien words, based on the pronounceable use of English. (What I mean to say is, the alien section has English words as the aliens themselves would speak it.) Have fun!

PARADISE PLANET OF SCHLOK

When Tnerb Robotics surveyed this region of space, naming the Ukopo Star in year 26, a Schlokan colony vessel had decrypted the survey data from Tnerb. A new course was reset to colonizing this secret planet.

A diverse planet of oceans, land, sky and life forms. Deemed a conservation planet from the start, construction is limited. The "footprint" of a building must climb from and bore into the soil, using depth and height in columns to reduce clearing of the natural landscape.

Capital of Schlok is Eloccan, which holds much promise, as a highland tower city with aqueducts rising over forests of Vlummm. Monorail access spans deep mines to Liagiba, in the south, and coastal tidal batteries generating power, in the north east.

Cousin Moons in the sky were settled as moon bases, Elleira and Adyak. They work in tandem with Schlok's Planetary Defence Force. Yelir and Mbaw, of the Outer Ring of the Ukopo System, have been honourable allies of Schlok for some time now.

"Our glorious planet will be deservedly protected. Schlok constitution passionately guards the rights of all life within the atmosphere."

-Schlok Embassy

ELLEIRA MOON BASE

Elleira was the first expansion from planet Schlok, 119 years ago, in year 92. A colony moon base of Schlok built to accommodate a barracks and a fleet of spacecraft at the star port. It has grown to specialize in medical research with an extensive technical workshop.

Void of an atmosphere, Elleira's surface boasts an impressive solar panel farm. Large power batteries are built underground. During the lunar day, solar panels harness the light, then power batteries trickle a power charge to keep the base running at night, until daylight regains base power.

Like its cousin moon Adyak, Elleira is also a listening post, noting any deficiencies on Ahtnamas. Prior to the Schlok invasion, saboteurs from Ahtnamas set five bombs on Elleira's oxygen generators. Three bombs were diffused, at last moment.

Communication ceased, soon after closing of a mass wedding on Schlok. Arrests were made. No casualties occurred. Elleira has an Orbital Defence Force Command Center, which investigates possible threats, or weaknesses in their own defence.

"An invasion of this magnitude warrants a counter
strike; may it bring the war to a quick end."

-Elleira Orbital Defence Force

ADYAK MOON BASE

In year 108, Adyak was established as the second expansion from planet Schlok. Like its cousin moon Elleira, Adyak is a military base. A listening post of radio antennae focus on Pwog, noting any deficiencies from Pwog's media chatter.

Both colonies of Schlok have star ports. The two moons have much traffic between them and planet Schlok. This creates an external economy, of which, Adyak has specialized in gourmet, quality processed food, for loading spacecraft for long voyages.

Adyak's auditorium is renowned for its cuisine and musical performances. You may, if lucky enough to attend, see popular bands from Eloccan, Liagiba, or even Yelir.

A team of saboteurs attempted to pollute the water supply, but fresh water was rerouted, flushing out the pollution. Firefights broke out between the saboteur team against Adyak's fearless respondents. The saboteur team is no more. Security measures were tightened with a formation of Adyak's Commando Regiment: ACR.

"No end to food and song at Adyak...Where the moon smiles."

-Adyak Auditorium

DESERT PLANET OF AHTNAMAS

An expansive race, which, as vast records indicate, first settled in year 85. A royal city called Suissak houses a royal hospital, academy, gardens, palace and citadel. Guardian Corporation manages the rest of Suissak. It is the only benevolent corporation on planet Ahtnamas. A secret underground rebel base is situated here.

The city of Mail, being the largest city off the planet Schlok, has descended into a police state fifteen years ago, since the Second Corporate War. Unfortunately, Ahtnamas had lost its true "gem" of a colony forty-four years ago, by surprise, in the First Corporate War. Amongst sand dunes, battles were fought near both cities in the past. Battles ended bitterly for the monarchy. Yet, Queen Ayam still rules Suissak.

Corporations in Mail have merged to form Mail Cartel. Secretly, having an alliance with Pwog. For as heavy of a blow the invasion on Schlok may be, the cartel must negotiate, through the Royal Family, with Schlok, or go into hiding.

"In a house divided, between those of us who value the return of order to our planet and those who want only the riches of this planet for themselves."

-Queen Ayam

BARREN PLANET OF REWWEX

Earliest records of dated artifacts place both Pwog and Rewwex at year 0, some 211 years ago. It has been speculated that separate settlements, settled at the same time, were a result of a space race, or a pioneering partnership gone wrong. It is known that there was a sudden loss of contact between the two colonies during their early development.

In any event, as sometimes factions may begin with good intentions, Rewwex grew cold enough to enslave any lone, or unsuspecting victims. If unlucky enough to be entangled in forced labour in the cold, dark mines under the colony of Nitram, then you would be less impressed with its terribly dark and intricate external facades on the surface structures.

Hall of Truth, in Rewwex Capital, justice and property rights of Rewwex owners are settled. Little empathy for life forms coincide with a commercial value for each individual's worth to the competing slavers.

Despite it all, Rewwex can be patient with others. They seldom interrupt each other. Rewwex are now on the defence against Schlok and its allies.

VOLCANIC PLANET OF PWOG

Having an atmosphere composed of sulphur-dioxide, Pwog has a sky in a constant drama, played out in extreme weather that includes frequent storms. Volcanic lava flow cools into flood plains of molten rock. A surface of brown silicate, with a rich iron-sulphide layer lying just under it's surface.

Pwog aggressively scheme with military science, mostly for its application of invading Schlok. For their dream is a dream of conquest, no matter how wasteful this may seem.

The pride of Pwog is their academy, in the capital of Notnarb, which trains its soldiers and officers to follow through with diabolical plans, for what most cultures would consider ridiculous.

Being that the planet Pwog, is extremely hostile, most scholars have predicted an end of Pwog by catastrophic events on their own planet. Holding up to their reputation, they send out attack, after attack, against Schlok. Pwog leadership tends to blame each other for their own military messes.

Astonishingly, some of the best music comes from Pwog; some say it's played too loud.

FROZEN PLANET OF YELIR

Originally, Yelir was a colony of technocrats that settled in the year 91. Orientated towards high technology, however useful, took second nature to a focus on arts and culture.

Famous for its studios, stages, restaurants and domed arena. Yelir boasts swim races in pools with audiences. This is widely broadcast. Yelir is a wealthy Federation, adopting many more social programs than most other colonies.

Having a nitrogen atmosphere, sunlight does not easily penetrate to the surface of Yelir. Wind turbines are plentiful on fringes of the colony. Capital of Yelir has a central financial district, surrounded by an extensive mining hub with garages full of tracked vehicles. Beyond that, outpost after outpost, most being rural communes producing product and services for Yelir Capital.

Situated near Yelir Capital is an abandoned colony left to ruin in year 103. A permit for salvage is available for application. Popular with prospectors, even alien beasts!

"Enemies of Schlok are enemies of Yelir."

-Federation of Yelir

MBAW MOON BASE

The only expansion of Yelir, established in year 105, Mbaw is the largest moon base in Ukopo Solar System.

With some protest, but no violence, Yelir released all holdings on Mbaw moon base, in return for a permanent alliance and an honour of officially recognizing their sovereignty as an emerging culture.

Mbaw has also forged an alliance with Schlok. Sharing embassies with Yelir off-moon. Using a common language and having a mutual respect, a partnership between Yelir and Mbaw has prospered. With Yelir's wealth and Mbaw's military and commercial star ports, a symbiotic relationship exists.

Being that Mbaw has no atmosphere, thus being a more hostile environment, Mbaw tends to emphasize a use of technology over the expression of the arts. Also, unlike Yelir, Mbaw has a sizable exploration fleet with a network of observatories capable of deep space surveying and a mapping of the heavens.

"It matters less how we fare from the invasion, rather where we direct our energies from here on."

-Unknown Mbaw Civilian

HAJILE STAR PORT

A stellar port founded seventy-three years ago in year 138, Hajile are a collection of aliens living in a commune that refuels spacecraft and gives all who come a good show. A theatre, fine dining and a concert hall are spectacular. The casino is a tourist trap.

Nice place to visit, wouldn't want to stay. Violence between the communists is rare, but there is constant bickering among them in a multitude of languages and gestures. A wrong gesture could insight a bunch of drama no one needs.

Although, Hajile star port has a fascinating facade, behind the scenes, communists prefer their district quite spartan. Hajile are craftsmen of industrial equipment. Surprisingly, produce a variety of perfume, as it is prized among them. Of course, if someone was to find a musk cologne, the colony may reconsider their neutrality and trade, or threaten you for it. Colognes are highly prized.

Hajile have harboured Rewwex, but despise Pwog.

"Rewwex are our misguided friends."

-Hajile Commune

TNERB ROBOTICS

Once an upstart exploration company, a Tnerb Deep-Space Exploration Probe had stumbled across a solar system with a dense mineral availability. Within it, several planets with major potential, especially, a deluxe planet teeming with life.

An attempt to keep this location a secret failed in year 26. Instead, establishing their Port at a safe region, beside an asteroid belt. In the wake of land grabs industry, trading and commerce excelled. Multiple construction projects were being commissioned, at a steady rate, for 185 years. Tnerb Robotics is one-part Star Port, Robotics Complex and Starcraft Production Facility.

Some might think this was accomplished overnight. It took time to endure, making progress this far. So, they like to celebrate. Often. Their multiple bay star port, or gigantic ship building facility, hardly impresses them, as much as, an army of robots that do battle in Tnerb arena.

Remote robot pilots with a variety of hero and villain profiles, trash talk each other, whilst regular events are broadcast wider than a Yelir soap opera. The Tnerb community is very fair, seeing all others as equals, except Pwog, who have attacked Tnerb before.

WERDNA VESSEL

The breech of the Werdna Vessel was nothing short of a small miracle. A small band of unknown pirates commandeered a deluxe starship of the Mountain Class three years ago.

A vessel which accommodates over one hundred berths, it can operate as a small Star Port. Unfortunately, the vessel's engine was heavily damaged. That made the ship vulnerable, until external mini-engines were fixed upon it, as well as, a massive cloaking device, which was commissioned within the first year of the breech.

It is not the vessel itself that is threatening, it is the Breech Pods designed to ram ships and penetrate a starcraft's hull, storming the ship with an assault team. Most of the time a breech procedure is a one-way trip, so an attack is either well prepared, or called off.

Little is known about Werdna community life. Except, that is about to change as Werdna leadership have recently sought infamy for their exploits. A small shuttle from Werdna Vessel has defected to Adyak recently. A press release will soon be broadcast, maybe amnesty granted for the crew onboard.

SECTION B - STORY INTRODUCTION

Within a dark pressurized cavern inside an isolated mining colony, on the planet of Rewwex, electric torches and shadows creep under vast mining equipment. "Replace the de-harmonizer before Thavek brings a Schlokan Ambassador, ugly one." Lorrque always put pressure on. Little sleep for slaves.

Voices carrying from the cavern tunnel stir Zod from off his woven mat. He rises, whilst wrapping his grotesque head, his skull cap rippled with gross growths.

"Halt, sir!" a kind feminine voice says from behind a weak spotlight shining on Zod's face. "Explain this total neglect of health code for this employee. He's suffering from fungicidal growth and multiple sulphur burns. I demand you to release this employee immediately for medical attention," Zoomie states bravely.

"As you wish, ambassador," booms Thavek, visibly angry at the request.

Without a glimpse at the female behind the voice, Zod is escorted to a Schlokan Shuttle.

Thavek continues, "Of course, the employee is now your responsibility."

"Of course, as it seems- you're not competent to have staff. I will be delivering my report to the Schlokan authorities. Farewell," Zoomie says, as she follows Zod into her shuttle.

"Have you experienced space travel yet?" Silence. "We will be up to a medical room in the mother ship in moments." Turning her beautiful face towards him, she rests her hands on his shoulders as tears roll down his face. "You're safe with us," whispers Zoomie.

In the soft glow of the medical room above, in a Schlokan mother ship, smells of delightful, pungent plants, each held by several crew members, are offered to Zod in his recovery. Zoomie especially enjoys the many book readings to her new near-mute, bandaged friend in recovery.

Nearly half way through the deep space voyage to the home planet of Schlok, time comes to remove Zod's head bandage. Zoomie's hands cup his cheeks. "Why, so handsome," Zoomie says with a smile. The crew then each offer hats from matter printers, that accept design programs and fabricate each unique hat.

Slowly, a tablet with Zod's self image is raised to his view. He breaks into a huge grin, trying on hats, as his comrades cheer, laughing happily.

Shortly after, Zod is standing beside their ship's large, tinted observation porthole and speaks into his recording device given to him from ship supply. His speech shifts between technical data, his life's journal and poetry in alien tongues of his previous owners.

Upon hearing the tongues he's spoken, Zoomie interrupts Zod. "You speak Rewwex, language of an original Ukopo race. A bunch of shifty slavers they are, but that is rare. Rare indeed."

Zod spends the day printing parts of a water ship from a matter printer. After assembly, the ship is encapsulated in a bottle, which is given to Zoomie as a surprise. Embossed on the crafted ship is a "δ", the first initial in her name, and Rewwex poetry dedicated to her. Her feelings of sincere joy focus directly on Zod.

Only a short time left before arriving on Planet Schlok, Zod takes Zoomie's hand. They walk the circular decks of the mother ship together. The corridors are lined with soft, illuminating panels. A silhouette is made as they share a long embrace.

Left alone together, Zoomie speaks in a soft voice. "It was a routine inspection at the mine, I never expected to fall in love with an alien male, who from what the surgeon says, is directly compatible with Schlokan anatomy. I would very much want to marry you Zod. I hope this is in agreement with customs of marriage that you may have as I never want to leave you."

Gently, Zod replies, "There are no customs from which I have been bound, even if I was bound by custom. I accept. We shall announce our love today."

Walking hand in hand through corridors of the ship, they hear applause erupt from informed crew members. Singles on Schlok plan a mass wedding planned for the next day, after the arrival on planet Schlok's Grand Gardens. Excitement on Schlok over wedding plans is paramount.

Has the eye ever fallen on falling dew, off a leaf in a bouquet of Vlummm; as is the day of the wedding. The day fleeting, like dew slipping, dripping off to the ground below.

This event is a passion of the inhabitants of Schlok. It represents a union of talents, a fusion of wills, of which, this planet had nurtured and pampered. Their celebration is as short lived as the day. For the next day will bring difficult choices, as the solar system is in great alarm.

It is custom to pick Vlummm on the planet of Schlok. Vlummm bouquets, full of squirming life forms, of many colours, are commonly carried on pillows, or draped over head pieces adorned by Schlokans.

Vlummm are more than beautiful vegetation, which are once a year brought to attend the mass weddings of Schlok and returned to the pastures, before the end of the evening.

Within Schlokan Grand Gardens, hundreds of attendees are dressed in brightly coloured, flowing garments. Each couple is brought from sunrise to sundown, before the crowds, to raise their hands up to the sky, blessing the day they declare their love.

Not much else is said. Ancient harps play melodies, with light drumming resonating from within the stadium. Pleasant sounds drift amidst the splendour of walking in groups around the gardens. Brief whispers of joy and acclamation can be heard.

Leaving grand gardens, arm in arm with Zoomie, Zod stands tall. His light blue form, like a giant puffed full of satisfaction. Zoomie's feminine form melts with her husband's embrace. The renowned pilot had never navigated her emotions about lifetime companionship. It is good.

Together, they enter the elevator delivering them to the depths of Schlok Undercity, to a life pod in the ambassador's stateroom. It was loaned, for tomorrow morning will bring back the pressures of a solar system on fire. **<<BEGIN>>**

SECTION C - BEGINNING CONTENT

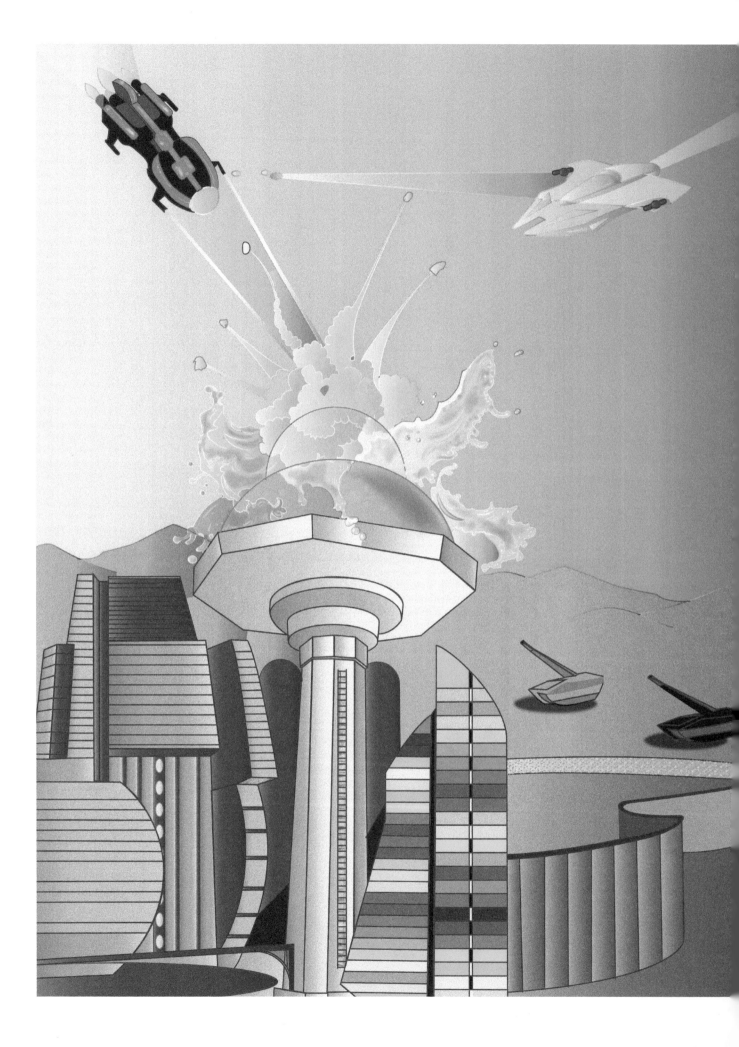

<<Begin>> Pleasant dreams evaporate, as caverns shake from blasts from the sky. Multiple laser beams aimed downward strike the fragile surface. Pulse cannons from unidentified military cruiser ships, in high orbit around Schlok's atmosphere, threaten the surface of the planet. Without a planetary force field, evacuation is difficult, maybe impossible.*

A) Take a sub-elevator to the supreme depths of Schlok's mining shafts to a Deep Bunker. An interplanetary distress call may be sent. Escape rockets have been installed from below.**<<A.25>>**

B) Take the monorail to the Liagiba Military Base on the surface of Schlok. From there, raise an army to evacuate to one of Schlok's moon bases on Elleira, or Adyak. (Both are moon bases well established on Schlok's two moons).**<<B.26>>**

C) Speed to the surface on a hangar elevator. Once there, commandeer a suitable transport vehicle to escape the atmosphere, evading the enemy fleet. Use a deep space scanning sensor, before launching out into the Ukopo solar system.**<<C.27>>**

<<A.25>> Crowded transport elevators full of civilians reach a Deep Bunker. After a short countdown over the speakers, the bunker is sealed. Holographic images pleading for inter-planetary rescue are made by various comrades. There is growing concern for a reply from the universe.*

A) Launch in an evacuation rocket heading for planet Ahtnamas (a neighbouring planet in the Ukopo solar system.) Providing the rocket's trajectory can run between the enemy fleet and an electro-magnetic field in Ukopo space quadrant.**<<A.28>>**

B) Stay in bunker. Send another round of rescue messages. Investigate banging sounds in bunker utility basement.**<<B.30>>**

<<B.26>> Upon reaching Liagiba Military Base, wounded and civilians have precedence for evacuation to Elleira. An army is unable to relocate. The battle remains on Schlok.

With a brief regroup, the standing army is poised for a counter-attack. Schlokan soldiers pillage the armoury, releasing recon drones shaped as oversized Schlokan insects to scout the atmosphere by the hundreds.*

A) Zod sets forth a plan to spread a formation of unenergized snipers, with heavy rifles, in a net with backup pulse mortars to knock out enemy power systems in their armour and ground vehicles. Brought forth from the armoury are many grey semi-automatic mass bullet rifles and elaborate pulse mortars with silver tubes on tripods.**<<A.32>>**

B) Zoomie decides to move as a regiment, pulling an arc towards the rear of the Pwog ground fleet, flanking the wounded enemy, and, of course, using as much speed as possible to force a manoeuvre on them. Zoomie pilots a Schlokan tracked vehicle to lead a cavalry of tracked vehicles over terrain well known to the Schlokan Regiment.**<<B.34>>**

<<C.27>> Using a hangar elevator to a surface hanger, walls of the elevator shake, as occupants rise in the magnetic elevator. As their portal opens, steam billows into their elevator. Zod leads into a hangar only to find all, but two spaceships have departed with civilians. Wounded and troops have fled to Elleira Moon Base.

A great opportunity awaits as both ships are fuelled and fully stocked. Being both an ambassador and a pilot, Zoomie must make a quick decision as to which one she wants to fly.*****

A) Choosing a transport shuttle with flights within the solar system and several light cannons, which are intimidating but require more frequent refuelling and provision stocking, Zoomie expects to level out over low altitudes. She follows the terrain, until making it to a safer side of the planet and climbs out of the atmosphere, out into the solar system.**<<A.40>>**

B) Deciding on a fuel tanker ship, with deep space engines and deep space life support capabilities, the pair may make their escape. Unfortunately, there is no fuel onboard to sell in the gas storage tank and no weapons. Only shield systems are available with a Tanker ship. Zoomie expects she may use anti-gravity engines to elevate far above the horizon, leaving the atmosphere. Only then can a deep scan of solar system be made with a space jump into Ukopo space.**<<B.36>>**

<<A.28>> Once they are seated in an escape rocket, its hatch is sealed. A short countdown is succeeded with a remarkable rumbling from their rocket's engines. A land portal opens to release the rocket up past the dreaded Pwog fleet, fruitlessly attempting to fire at the rocket. Defence flares fire as the rocket spirals out of the atmosphere, into space.

Their voyage to Ahtnamas is cramped. A brief hibernation sleep allows for it to be tolerable. Making it to Ahtnamas, they soar above, in Ahtnamas's carbon-dioxide atmosphere. Two radio channels open to accept landing by parachute. Zod must decide which radio channel to accept.*****

A) Choosing a Mail space port channel, a parachute is deployed, their rocket descends to its port's launch pad. Once the rocket's hatch is opened, the pair assemble onto the launch pad. Pwog soldiers begin to surround their pad. Lorrque shouts at Zod, "We meet again."**<<A.38>>**

B) Choosing a Royal channel on Suissak, an immediate answer from Thavek responds, "All fleeing Schlokan vessels are to be destroyed!" Zod immediately deploys a parachute, illegally landing the rocket on Ahtnamas's desert-like terrain. They are now stranded in an arid Ahtnamas desert with a thick CO_2 atmosphere.**<<B.41>>**

<<B.30>> Using the bunker's basement hatch, Zoomie and Zod descend to caverns below. Vlummm surrounds an underground pool. From within the pool, an oversized beast emerges with a grey-blue coat of fur and four horns curling from her head. The creature telepathically speaks.

"Yes, my children, Pwog is here to harm us. They are assisted by Rewwex. They have met their match. They must pay. They are desperate, knowing that their army is small, and realizing our messages will be heard beyond the deaf ears of Ahtnamas...protect Vlummm." *****

A) Zod attempts to converse with the beast by way of the mind such questions as: "Who are you, what should we do about the invasion and how do you speak our language?" **<<A.42>>**

B) Zoomie attempts to converse with the beast by way of a universal translator adorned on her neck. She asks questions, such as: "Who are you, where should we strike at Pwog and how can you speak telepathically?" **<<B.43>>**

<<A.32>> Using a sniper net and pulse mortar tactic, a Schlokan Army neutralizes an invading Pwog ground force. Once, Zod leads the snipers to their positions and opens fire with unenergized rifles, power suits of Pwog deflect the projectiles.

Zoomie orders five stations of pulse mortars to fire from behind combat trenches. All mechanized armour and vehicles come to a halt. Many prisoners are rounded up as the invasion is suppressed. Now the pair must decide as what to do with the successful manoeuvre.*****

A) The duo decides to methodically capture, collecting prisoners into an underground Schlokan prison. Once there, Zoomie may humanely interrogate Pwog soldiers for information regarding details of invasion plans, thus gathering intelligence on Pwog leadership.**<<A.44>>**

B) The duo decides to trade Pwog prisoners to Mail, on the planet of Ahtnamas, as per requested, on a basis of a newly-formed partial cease-fire agreement. Wherein, some regions of Ukopo space, near Schlok, will be safe from enemy movement now. In return, all prisoners of Schlok will be freed immediately.**<<B.45>>**

<<B.34>> Leading a cavalry of tracked vehicles behind the enemy, Zoomie starts to lose the chase. Pwog's 4X4 and 6X6 wheeled vehicles are in the distance and gain enough space to abandon their vehicles in their retreat, boarding a Pwog transport ship.

Zoomie prepares a missile on the top of their tracked vehicle, while Zod inputs coordinates, launching a missile above, creating a fantastic explosion above in the Schlokan sky. The transport ship doesn't leave the atmosphere.

Zoomie sends Schlok Command a message to retrieve Pwog's abandoned vehicles for research. Zod says, "Such a pity we should find ourselves a bitter spoil of war. When will Pwog ever learn peace?"

Once they return to Liagiba base, they see a pitiful view of casualties lying under medical tents, situated within the gates of the base. They are being ferried by drone stretchers. The scene, for them, is deeply humbling. *

A) Zoomie's hot-line to Schlok Embassy, on her tablet, suggests seeking passage to a cousin moon base. Also, it encourages them to join a counteroffensive that will best capture Rewwex, or de-rail any Pwog aggression.

Zod reserves a berth cabin for Elleira aboard a transport that is leaving before dark. They sway with exhaustion as they board the ship, washing up to return to a desperate base. Then they help the wounded, until their ship calls for boarding.**<<A.46>>**

B) As their damaged track vehicle limps into the base, a soldier yells, "There is a spare berth available headed for Adyak. Get out and RUN to it. It's leaving NOW!" Jumping out, they run towards the boarding call from the ship.

They use every bit of strength to wade through many wounded lying in stretchers on the ground. Zod stumbles on the on-ramp to the departing transport ship. They both laugh at their desperation, boarding on time.**<<B.47>>**

<<B.36>> Where does one take a fuel tanker in this quadrant of the universe? To a gas supply depot at Hajile star port, of course, where gas is cheap and plentiful. It sits on an interstellar crossroads.

Zoomie and Zod are receiving messages in a glow of the tanker's cockpit. Pwog have retreated, meaning the Invasion of Schlok has been suppressed. Pwog's small space fleet has been bested. No further damage should befall Schlok by these villains.

As they approach the great refuelling nests, a signal guides their ship into a large fuelling nozzle, where a catwalk is deployed, interconnecting the airlock. Zoomie leads with a laser pistol behind her back. A thick metal robot in grey, with red accents speaks.

"Welcome traders. Gambling, dining and theatre are available attractions!" Neither of them gamble, so they decide to either…*****

   A) Go out to dine on a date. They would then set course back to Adyak, returning the ship. This would give their home planet a boost with a heavily anticipated fuel load.

   With several restaurants to choose from, Zoomie picks a small dimly-lit booth seated alongside a grill.

   A yellow, four-armed chef makes up harvested aquatic creatures in distinctly flavoured batter, tossing them onto the grill with fireballs. Flash fires sear the food.

   Zod says, with a laugh, "That was quick. Great choice. Fast food that tastes a little smokey."**<<A.48>>**

   B) Go out to a theatre. They would then set course for Mbaw Moon Base. It pays dearly for fuel and is an enemy of Rewwex.

   The magnificent domed theatre houses a diverse audience, which watch actors tell a foreign story by performance. An interpreter tells the story to Zoomie and Zod. The audience marvels at the plot, surprised by mock laser battles and poetic moments of the act. Thoroughly impressed, they spend hours discussing the act, cherishing the moment, before departing for Mbaw.**<<B.49>>**

<<A.38>> Seldom is ultra-fury witnessed of Zod, but after nine Pwog guards have been shot with Zod's ray gun rifle, Lorrque realizes that fleeing is an option.

As Zod runs, ducking between well aimed shots at Pwog soldiers, Zoomie runs with her magnetic boots, up diagonally, to the catwalk above the launch pad. Closing in on Lorrque's position, Zoomie pulls herself over the rail, donning her power whip, entangling Zod's former slaver unto the walkway. "Nooooo!" pleads Lorrque.

Once in custody, Lorrque begs Zod not to harm him. Zod breathes deeply, "We must protect Vlummm. You're going to jail on Schlok."

"And, I will see that he gets there. Greetings, heroes of Schlok, welcome to Ahtnamas. Glad you both could show up for the party. I have an antique shuttle available for you to use in your pursuit of our enemy! After all, I am Nezto, leader of Ahtnamas Rebels. Unfortunately, Thavek has escaped."

<<D.55>>

<<A.40>> As Zoomie examines instructions from Schlok Embassy, it is clear the transport shuttle is full of advanced starcraft components. The cargo must be given to Tnerb Robotics, to trade for, a Ranger Class vessel.

This deep space exploration vessel has twin torpedo tubes, several laser turrets and a belly hold with a high performance tracked vehicle.

An encrypted message includes the bounties of Rewwex officers. Also, a license to stop Pwog at all costs, within the limits of Ukopo Solar System. Congratulations is given to survivors of an Invasion of Schlok.*

  A) Course is set for Tnerb Robotics. Enroute, Zod applies for a Tnerb Robot Fighting Tournament, reserving a robot rental for Zoomie to pilot. Zoomie asks, "How are you going to operate a pilot console Zod?" "I am not. You are!" They share a laugh. **<<A.50>>**

  B) Course is set for Tnerb Robotics. A faint distress signal, on the way, becomes increasing stronger, until a hazard alert sounds. A large invisible object appears as a Mountain Class vessel.

  Zoomie sends out a recognition signal of peace. Zod says to Zoomie, "We better dock and meet our new neighbours. Something tells me that we won't get past it alone." So, a docking request is made. **<<B.51>>**

<<B.41>> Before panic can set in, because of a limited breathing supply within their suits. Zod sends a boosted signal as he rigs the radio components together. Within moments, a red tracked vehicle with a single mass cannon and many laser turrets drives by, stopping suddenly. A rear airlock door opens as a ramp. No choice but to go inside.

With guns drawn, the pair waits for the portal to open. Four Royal Guards stand branding stun batons. Behind them, a beautiful Ahtnamas Queen is sitting, smiling, gesturing for them to join her. They sit beside her porthole, as her tracker jerks forward, beginning to crawl.

Ayam says curtly, "So, if I was to take you to my Royal Star Port and permit your use of one of three of my Royal Cruisers, would you chase Thavek back to Yelir? You are to capture that instigator. Am I right?" Zoomie glances at Zod, as they smile with anticipation. **<<D.57>>**

<<A.42>> A warm feeling falls over their minds, as a channel of dreaming begins to show a Pwog base on Rewwex, a Ranger vessel docked on the ground landing pad, beautiful Vlummm and the beast giving whispers of "Emor, goddess of Vlummm."

Waking, the duo take an elevator to a tunnel, reaching an airlock adjacent to the landing pad. Zoomie casts doubt with saying, "I see not a ship Zod. What are we to do?"

At that same moment, a Tnerb Ranger Class vessel lands with a sweeping motion. A tube-shaped vessel appears commanding, as legs lower beneath the starcraft. Slowly, a ramp lowers. The ship's crew summon them to board.

Onboard, they are greeted by pirates, the renowned Werdna crew. "We are here to pick you up. We will be taking you to Rewwex, in accordance with Emor's wishes," says Captain Tanz-Buk-Hool. **<<D.59>>**

<<B.43>> With a song in perfect Schlok language, it begins,

"You speak to Emor...a goddess, protector of Vlummm. To Notnarb, you must come. Where they train, in their barracks, a flood doth rain, sweeping their conquest dreams away."

"It has been, since Schlok was young, to forget the old language and adopt a new one."

"Our language is the language of Vlummm, my child, now see yourself to the tunnels. See to it our quest is done."

Emor disappears into the pool, as water begins to flood into their chamber. A river rises through the tunnel. An open hole gaping in the ceiling of the cavern becomes accessible. They float on a wave, pulling themselves through the hole to the surface.

Nearby, an abandoned Saucer Starcraft had settled, wedged between jagged rocks. The pair enter the foreign vessel. Zoomie says, "I haven't seen these controls before."

Zod says earnestly, "Relax...hold this globe. Use your mind to operate this ship." Then they fall into a hibernation sleep. The Saucer Starcraft begins their journey to Notnarb.**<<D.61>>**

<<A.44>> Once contained in Schlok's underground prison, prisoners are cleaned, outfitted and fed. With exception of the wounded, each Ahtnamas prisoner had few stories. Pwog have none. Concentrating on Rewwex officers, Zoomie finds out Pwog have an armoury of 6X6 armoured vehicles on a remote place located on the barren planet of Rewwex. Also, Zod finds out the bases coordinates from tired, restless soldiers.

An urgent message from Schlok Embassy orders Zoomie to have prisoners released to Mail, on the desert planet of Ahtnamas. Zod begins to organize prison shuttles as Zoomie has a word with Rewwex officers. "We shall see a new Rewwex emerge now. Annexation policies are now in effect. Rewwex is about to be carved up in land grabs...you poor sods."

Transferring command of the prisoners, the pair leave for a surface hanger to board a transport shuttle to Tnerb Star Port, expecting to transfer starcraft, for the second leg of the journey. Their new destination is to the coordinates of a "secret" Pwog vehicle armoury on Rewwex.**<<D.63>>**

<<B.45>> As they descend into a carbon-dioxide atmosphere of Ahtnamas at night, Mail's landing pads are illuminated with lights. Welcoming back its soldiers in a war fought, and lost, for Mail's corporate power in the solar system. Zoomie leads Zod to a port lobby, where they see for themselves sensitive reunions of families and lovers.

"Oh Zod, war tears apart families. Deaths leave the loved ones in despair. We must learn to prevent this," Zoomie says. Zod agrees.

Within an inner lobby, a small-formed cloaked figure snatches some cargo from a basket. The pair give chase. Upon reaching the figure, Zod pulls the dark cloak back to reveal a frightened Ahtnamas female, begging to be released from punishment of theft.

At this moment, lights in the corridor go out. An electro-net drops from the ceiling, entangling them. Lights from assault weapons shine on their faces. The lead corporate officer says sternly, "Tell the Embassy to negotiate with Mail Cartel. On this planet, we rule. Don't forget this. You're released."**<<D.65>>**

<<A.46>> Conference calls to loved ones, helping wounded civilians and a military meeting consume their time during a short trip to Elleira. It is apparent, an annexation of Rewwex will commence, meaning that Rewwex territory is limited. Property purchases will be available on Rewwex.

Zoomie opens up. "Now land grabs will motivate everyone against our aggressors. Being a barren planet, it has something everyone wants."

"A breathable atmosphere," Zod chirps.

They then suit up to arrive at the landing strip of Elleira Moon Base. Without entering the base, they transfer to a Ranger Class vessel, equipped with torpedoes. The crew settles into a berth onboard a legendary starcraft heading to Rewwex. It is Schlok Command which is mounting a counteroffensive to secure the capital city of Rewwex first.

Getting to Rewwex is dangerous as there are conflicts expected enroute. The crew spends time researching maps of Ukopo, as well as using Zod's captivity to describe the inner workings of Rewwex infrastructure. Sharing this with their comrades as they near Rewwex space.**<<D.67>**

<<B.47>> Once aboard, they wash, eat and sleep in their berth. Waking, Zoomie is surprised to find the moon of Adyak far behind them. "Where are we going?" asks Zoomie.

Zod speaks gently, "We were fleeing several Pwog attack drones. We are headed for Tnerb Robotics for an upgrade to a Ranger Class vessel. I have been awake for a lunar night... just watching you sleep well. You've been out awhile."

After doing research on Tnerb, Zoomie states, "I want to battle in the arena at Tnerb, I want to challenge myself here."

But, time does not allow them that luxury, as they are ushered to the next starcraft. Onboard, there's a military meeting to discuss area targets for a seek and capture mission. Concentrating the mission on rural Rewwex, outside the capital city.

Any loyalist to Rewwex would be fitted a harmless tracer button, adhered to the back of their neck, until an allied officer would have it removed at the future Head Quarters. A Head Quarters in an occupied Rewwex capital city. Soon to be known as New Rewwex. They relax for the rest of the voyage in privacy.**<<D.69>>**

<<A.48>> Leaving Hajile Star Port, Zoomie receives a transmission from Schlok Embassy. It requests them to deliver fuel to a remote fuel depot on Rewwex instead. A way point is given to meet with escort starcraft in Rewwex space. Zoomie accepts.

Zod pulls her aside, saying kindly, "You know I trust your judgment, but that journey is mostly un-escorted."

"If we go through a hollow in the magnetic belt in Ukopo space, we can take an out-of-the-way route and still beat waiting for another escort," Zoomie replies.

Their journey through spaces awesomely dangerous electro-magnetic belt goes well, as Zoomie had predicted. Except the starcraft are not at the arranged spot. What's worse the communication equipment is not properly amplifying signals to properly communicate at a distance.

Zod references maps to coordinate a route in order to end up at the Fuel Depot on time. Zoomie agrees, saying with a laugh, "If we get to the depot on time, you owe me a dinner date. If we don't, you still owe me a dinner date." **<<D.71>>**

<<B.49>> "To see Mbaw's base structures lit up from above, during a lunar night, takes my breath away!", Zoomie exclaims with awe. As their fuel tanker hovers above glowing webs of pyramids, cubes, towers and landing pads, a signal guides them to the right launch pad to touchdown on.

Once in the lobby, bunches of kids surround them with their parents cheering, "Welcome to our rock in the sky. We welcome the survivors of the invasion!" The sentiment is appreciated, but a calm had reached them, knowing that it could have been their end.

The fuel tanker broker gives Zoomie and Zod massive forms of credit in Yelir currency, which is the most prized in the Ukopo system. The fuel broker gets serious. "I am Jneese...There is something I must tell you. Thavek is located now on Yelir. In Yelir's abandoned colony of ruins. He plots to store Pwog weapons beneath our nose."

Zod replies. "If you are who you say you are, if Thavek is where you say he is, then you have made a very happy friend." The two men hold each other's elbows, as is the custom of an alliance between males on Mbaw.**<<D.73>>**

<<A.50>> As the shuttle approaches a massive Tnerb space port, a signal guides them into a honey comb landing pad in the inner wall of the large port. As the shuttle settles, a clear wall shuts in the bay. Atmosphere returns to breathable within it. A dormant robot standing tall in the bay, with a manifest attached, reading, "When the sun sets, Tnerb Arena begins one-on-one robot battles."

Zod begins to make upgrades of thigh mounted smoke canister launchers and a back piece that hurls an electro-net backwards. Zoomie tweaks combat controls to fine settings. She also uses mind medium hardware to link her mind with the robot telepathically, as suggested by Zod. With only moments to practice with the remote console, the robot shows an agility with tremendous strength. They ferry the robot through the service tunnel to the arena, already loud with chanting battle songs and applause.

"Nervous, Zoomie? You shouldn't be. It's not everyday we can bet against Mail Cartel's robot, 'Crater Maker.'"

Zoomie says back to Zod, "With our 'Liagiba Survivor,' we can't lose."**<<D.75>>**

<<B.51>> A docking request is replied to swiftly, as a signal guides them to a side of the ship. A catwalk extends to the belly ramp, encapsulating it for a sealed connection. As a gate opens, stylish aliens in black leathers posture with cannon guns drawn, but their guns are raised upwards.

"I am Hool-Bu-Teel. We welcome you to Werdna Vessel. As you can see the interior is cramped, as we are collecting every damn piece of Vlummm, from Elloccan to Liagiba. I'm just glad it moves aside to let us pass."

Zoomie laughs. The interior of the corridors is beautifully lined with Vlummm. "I take it you are trying to save Vlummm, as a precaution, because of the invasion?," asks Zod.

"Emor, goddess of Vlummm, predicted the invasion. We just done our part," Hool-Bu-Teel says. As the group enter the inner lobby, an alert calls out over the intercom to occupy stations, as a Pwog Cruiser is in their vicinity.

"Should we be afraid?" asks Zod. Some of Werdna crew chuckle as they start to gear up to occupy Breech Pods in preparations for an attack on a Pwog Cruiser.**<<D.77>>**

SECTION D - CONCLUDING CONTENT

<<D.55>> Ahtnamas Rebels lead them to an adjacent landing strip with the most beat up, old transport shuttle on the planet. As they settle into the antique vessel, Lorrque explains to them, at Hajile Commune, a system of doing things in their space port, which harbours Rewwex, including storage of their weapons.

The plan is called "The Circuit." Lorrque is given a berth. He is put on full time watch during the voyage to Hajile star port. Zoomie hails Hajile, providing evidence to the counsel, in which, they fully concede, admitting their allegiance to Rewwex. Zoomie speaks softly, "We are on our way. Remember, supporters of slavers are supporters of slavery."

Upon their arrival, a celebration of an abolishment of slavery is in full swing. A theatrical musical performance is dedicated to freed slaves within Ukopo Solar System. Schlok Embassy broadcasts an end to the war, over speakers, to a grateful crowd. Cheers resound, as Zod is raised above a crowd. Zoomie holds her cheeks, unable to stop smiling. They then embrace, sharing a kiss. It feels like it last forever.

End. Go to page 25.

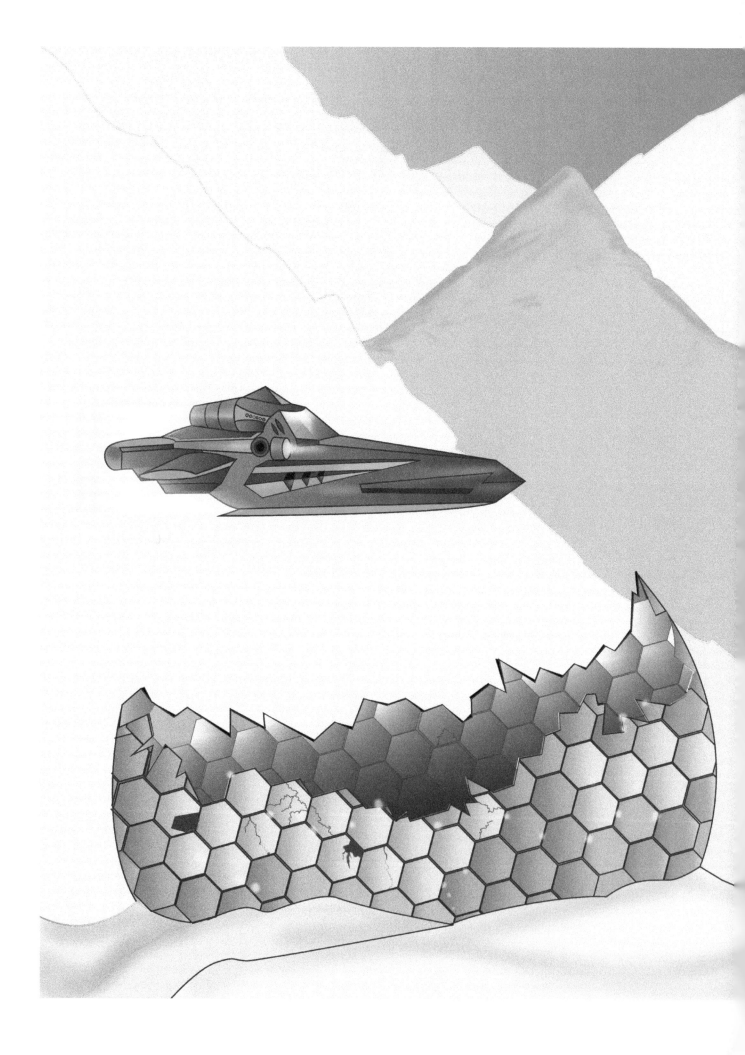

<<D.57>> Once inside the Royal Cruiser, Queen Ayam gives an official bounty on Thavek, before departing swiftly. Their ship rises, as Zoomie sets course for Yelir to ambush Thavek at an abandoned colony. A famous royal spy ring had provided them information.

A tremendous space jump soon brings them within Yelir near orbit. Descending, Zod wishes her the best. Zoomie lands them into an abandoned, roofless Bio-Dome. Donning their suits, they advance to an energized portion of the colony. Zod drills a fibre optic scope into a wall beside the hatch.

Seeing Thavek's company quarrelling, a small Pwog squad board a Pwog Scout Shuttle with Thavek leading them inside.

"We won't be able to chase him back," claims Zod.

"Look, Zod! At the adjacent holds, we have found a Pwog armoury of weapons. I am calling it in!" exclaims Zoomie.

Yelir Orbital Patrol releases them, taking over the crime scene. The pair are shuttled back to Yelir capital with a hero's welcome. An announcement of the end of the war is played over an intercom. They enjoy admiration of a talented collection of artists who greet them with compliments for their sense of duty. The couple smiles and waves.

End. Go to page 25.

<<D.59>> Werdna crew shows great prowess in navigating their way to Rewwex. Drawing the Ranger Class vessel into a tracking orbit pointing towards the surface of Rewwex, they try to find a Pwog Robotics Complex.

Zod states boldly, "Ready pulse torpedoes."

Zoomie, whose head is in the targeting view finder, follows with, "Permission to fire?"

"Fire!" shouts Tanz-Buk-Hool.

In one direct hit, a cloud of blue energy expands and implodes, leaving a confused Pwog Army with over a hundred robot warriors with fried internal components. Once landed, their crew rushes a small complex, surrounding a dazed defence platoon.

A Mbaw cruiser sends in an occupation force to relieve them, investigating the scene. The couple are shuttled to the cruiser above them, to find many hugs and much cheering from many Mbaw passengers. Werdna crew are also recognized as heroes, which is new in Ukopo history.

Zod hugs Zoomie, hearing over speakers that an accord of peace has been official in the quadrant. Zod says, "There is enough scrap back there, at that complex, to build us a fine dwelling!"

Zoomie replies, "Anywhere with you, Zod!"

End. Go to page 25.

<<D.61>> Waking, in near orbit of a dangerous planet of Pwog, Zoomie stirs Zod awake. She asks, "What do we do when we get there?"

He replies, "With only one laser cannon, I would suggest attacking the colony's water tower, next to the Academy Barracks."

They tense up, as the saucer dives towards Notnarb. It's seemingly impossible to lock onto the target, but Pwog Academy comes into view. Zoomie clusters lasers on one point of the tower ball. It explodes, with water spilling over to the soil. The return fire is fierce at the Saucer Starcraft, yet it escapes above the atmosphere. While enroute to Rewwex, a transmission from Schlok Embassy declares an end of the war in Ukopo space quadrant.

They hold hands, while exiting their saucer that had landed in a field, by Hall of Truth, in Rewwex capital city. Crowds of allied soldiers cheer their arrival. One soldier from Elleira shouts, "I guess both of you are to blame for putting Notnarb on alert. Fearing an invasion, Pwog have lost their will to fight!"

Zoomie says, "I think the fight is out of everyone. Just remember, our treatment of our enemy will now determine if we will have to fight each other again."

End. Go to page 25.

<<D.63>> In Tnerb Star Craft Facility, both Zoomie and Zod are amazed, as their transport is upgraded to a Tnerb Dronecraft. An egg-shaped craft with many landing gears. It is capable of remotely operating two attack drones. "A pilot's dream craft!" says Zoomie, as they board with command of the ship and its crew.

The Dronecraft makes a space jump to Rewwex near orbit. Zoomie sets herself at the console, with one other pilot, launching attack drones at Pwog Armoury. Several laser cannons strafe over the exiting 6X6 vehicles, whilst guided missiles weave into the Pwog hanger, laying the contents to waste. A surrender plea is made by a Pwog Armoured Sargent. Before Zoomie can accept, Schlok Embassy broadcasts an official peace accord within Ukopo space.

Adyak Commando Regiment meets their crew on the surface of Rewwex. An impromptu party begins with song and dance. The couple join the dance and close with a slow dance among cheers.

Many newly-made songs commemorate the couple's part in the victory over Pwog. It is the best dance of theirs lives. It is not their last.

End. Go to page 25.

<<D.65>> Once the three untangle themselves from a de-energized net, the female "decoy" runs back to the lobby. Zod says, while pulling out a pouch of powder, "Let's track them!" Using small pinches, the powder reveals foot prints. Foot prints lead them to a portal, in which, Zod drills a fibre optic scope into the wall.

The fibre optic scope reveals a large meeting of Mail Cartel's leadership. Zoomie produces a sleeping disc, capable of making a gas cloud that puts, those in the cloud, to sleep. Zod then rigs the door console, defeating a locking mechanism. As the portal opens, Zoomie tosses a disc along the floor. Zod shuts in the portal quickly.

Zoomie says with urgency, "It is about time I let Ahtnamas Rebels know where these nasty guys sleep, for when they wake up, it will be in jail."

As anticipated, Rebels come with no delay, fastening braces and tracers to each wealthy prisoner.

Nezto, the leader of the Rebels speaks, "Did you hear the news? Schlok Embassy has declared a system-wide peace."

Applause breaks out, as Zod kisses Zoomie, softly saying, "There is nothing that can come between our love. It is stronger than an invasion."

End. Go to page 25.

<<D.67>> Sensors on their Ranger Vessel pick up a Pwog assault squadron approaching, as they near Rewwex. Torpedoes fire quickly, damaging their enemy's engines. Undeterred, their Ranger vessel enters the atmosphere, landing by an abandoned slave barracks in city centre.

Advancing to the basement, Schlokan Squad moves in sequence, on alert, with sounds of a firefight on the streets. Entering a tunnel connected to the Hall of Truth, they encounter stark resistance from Rewwex Elite Guards. The guards are bested by advanced urban combat tactics of Schlokan Squad. Before breaching a command control portal, a stand down is called. A radio channel claims total surrender of Pwog and Rewwex, as conveyed from Schlok Embassy. The portal opens to find a gathering of collaborators of the Schlok invasion walking out, unarmed, in disgrace.

Schlokan Squad secures the scene. Zod raises Zoomie to his shoulder, parading her around outside, in city centre, among crowds celebrating the liberation.

Zoomie shouts to the crowd, "To Schlok and its allies, we salute you for our liberty. We protected Vlummm!"

Zod confidently raises her even higher in the air. Well above the crowd.

End. Go to page 25.

<<D.69>> No resistance on the journey to Rewwex, as radio chat indicates an Allied "sweep" of this region, allowing for safe passage through this part of Ukopo space. Zoomie scans Rewwex terrain surrounding its capital. Many unarmed heat signatures are found with their warm bodies covered in rags. Calling in coordinates for pickup of individuals, leading them to find a cluster of Pwog assault and transport starcraft about to launch.

Zod says calmly, "Call in our findings, as I doubt, they could run far without giving up."

At this moment, Schlok Command orders them to stand down, as the official declaration of peace is transmitted over the radio channel. Schlok Embassy also, commends the reconnaissance of the region for saving lives, as well as, avoiding unwanted destruction.

Their vessel docks in a fuel depot, on the edge of Rewwex, beside many tents of refugees. Plenty of them are former slaves.

"Have hope, for a brand-new world is here for us now, to share with each other. To learn to get along with each other, despite our differences!" shouts Zoomie as she kisses Zod in front of a cheering crowd.

End. Go to page 25.

<<D.71>> Before the fuel tanker enters Rewwex atmosphere, Zod realizes the destination was his old mining colony of Nitram, a slave mine set abreast a citadel on the surface of a purple mountain range. A radio channel opens. Zod begins to talk to the ground control, at Nitram.

Zod says, "Mechanics have made it to the colony. It is a free colony, after a brutal uprising over the previous slavers. We are welcome."

Zoomie then descends to land on a landing pad surrounded by an assortment of junky spacecraft. Groups of Rewwex slaves huddle around bonfires for warmth.

"Bring out the fuel hoses! Get these ships to a hospital in the capital," says the Mbaw mechanics. Sincere accolades are given to the pair on their arrival.

Zod retreats back to their tanker, returning with bundles of delicious frozen aquatic creatures to eat. Approaching Zoomie at a bonfire, Zod says, "About that dinner date?"

A crowd cheers, as the radio announces the end of the war. Zoomie exclaims, "I love you Zod!" They hold hands, breaking into old songs of victory and remembrance.

End. Go to page 25.

<<D.73>> Jneese sets the two up with a Hunter Class ship. They depart for an abandoned colony on Yelir. As their ship approaches the colony, a Pwog scout shuttle takes off so close, that Thavek is seen within the shuttle. Zoomie swings the hunter ship behind the scout shuttle, applying a tractor beam.

Neither vessel can move. Zod hails Thavek's shuttle warning Thavek to surrender. The scout ship deploys a de-harmonizer, breaking the bond, escaping, after dropping their payload. Zoomie says, "The de-harmonizer has scrambled our instruments, we can't chase him, but we can grab the payload."

They soon arrive at Yelir Capital with payload in tow. Once grounded, a payload opens from within a pressurized ship bay in Yelir. The payload reveals five captured high-ranking Yelir officers. Colonists cheer with appreciation, as each officer is greeted and returned home.

The end of the war is announced from Yelir Command. An instance of joy resounds, as colonists greet the couple with attention.

Zod says, "Five good reasons to travel the quadrant with you Zoomie." Zoomie then replies, "You are the only reason I need!"

End. Go to page 25.

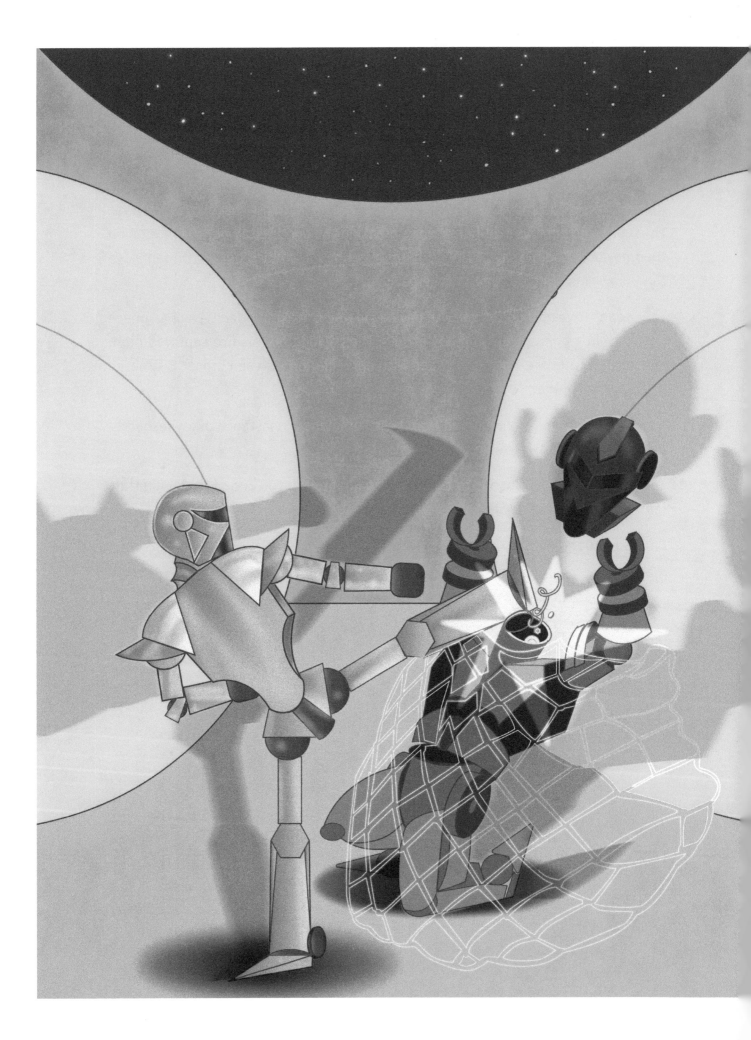

<<D.75>> A marquee wrapping around Tnerb Arena states eight to one odds against Liagiba Survivor. Millions of credits at stake, with an ecstatic crowd, a horn goes off. The pair of robots charge each other. Liagiba Survivor is immediately tossed into several walls by the Maker. Launching smoke, the Survivor manages to pin the Maker against the wall, back to back, with Crater Maker facing the wall. Liagiba Survivor deploys an electro-net from its back.

Crater Maker is trapped against the wall, so Liagiba Survivor runs along the circumference of the wall, its feet on the wall and plants a tremendous kick, taking the head clean off Crater Maker. The Survivor raises the robotic head to the crowd, to the roar of victory applause.

Immediately, Mail Cartel representatives are rounded up to facilitate a recovery of a fantastic wager lost by Mail Cartel.

Zoomie exclaims, "Proceeds will be donated to *real* survivors in Liagiba! Vlummm continues to grow on Schlok!"

Zod perches Zoomie on his shoulders, walking around the arena, holding his hero tightly. An official peace accord is announced over the speakers to an enthusiastic applause.

End. Go to page 25.

<<D.77>> A spherical Breech Pod slams into a Pwog Cruiser, embedding partially into its hull, sealing itself with chemical sealant. As its pod hatch opens, two three-wheeled drones take to the corridors. Hool-Bu-Teel shouts, "Sweep left!" A Werdna rear guard places a plasma wall generator to the right, sealing off the corridor. Werdna crew engage a Pwog Defence Platoon expertly.

A "Jacker" sets up at each door, overriding it to open. Progress through the interior of the ship finds thirteen Pwog bested, with no casualties for Werdna crew. The crew finally makes it to the belly hold, to find countless treasures obtained from Rewwex, as it was payment for the weapons produced by Pwog.

Zoomie says, "A treasure ship, with more wealth than most."

Zod replies, "This treasure was born from blood and suffering of Rewwex people. We shall see it returned to impoverished people of Rewwex."

Werdna crew are reluctant, but accept the protest in kind. Upon heading the Pwog Cruiser back to Werdna Vessel, an announcement is made for an accord of peace in the Ukopo Solar System. Zoomie squeezes Zod's hand, saying, "Even the pirates know what you said is right. Another reason why I love you!"

End. Go to page 25.

SECTION 6 - APPENDIX

GLOSSARY

- academy – place of study, or training in a special field.

- acclamation – loud and eager assent to a proposal.

- accommodate – provide lodging, or room for.

- ambassador – representative, or promoter of a specified thing.

- amnesty – a general pardon for offences.

- anti-gravity engine – engine that defies gravity.

- arid – too dry to support vegetation: barren.

- ascertain – find out as a definite fact.

- asteroid(s) – any of the small planetary bodies revolving around the star.

- astonishingly – amaze.

- atmosphere – the envelope of gases surrounding the planet.

- auditorium – part of a theatre etc., in which, the audience sits.

- benevolent – well meaning and kindly.

- berth – a fixed bunk on a ship, train, etc., for sleeping in.

- bickering – quarrel pettily; wrangle.

- breach – break through; make a gap in.

- cartel – a group of manufacturers, or suppliers, with a purpose of maintaining prices at a high level and controlling production, marketing arrangements, etc.

- catastrophic event – a great and usually sudden disaster.

- citadel – a fortress, usually built on high ground, protecting a city.

- cloaking device – a device which conceals something.

- cologne – a dilute solution of alcohol and a concentrate of perfume.

- commandeer – take possession without authority.

- commission – bring into operation.

- commune – a group of people who live together and share responsibilities, possessions, etc.

- communist – a person advocating, or practising communism.

- companionship – good fellowship; friendship.

- compatible – able to co-exist; well suited.

- competent – adequately qualified, or capable.

- comrade – a workmate, friend, or companion.

- conservation – preservation, especially of the natural environment.

- constitution – the body of fundamental principles, or established precedents according to which a state is acknowledged to be governed.

- constitutional monarchy – a nation whose official head of state is a king, or queen, with powers that are limited by a nation's constitution.

- converse – engage in conversation.

- corporation – a group of people authorized to act as an individual and recognized in law as a single entity.

- custom – a traditional and widely accepted way of behaving, or doing something that is specific to a particular society, place, or time.

- deaf – wholly, or partly without hearing.

- deemed – regard, consider, or judge.

- deficiency – a fault, or weakness in something, or someone, that makes it, or them, less successful.

- de-harmonizer – electronic scrambler.

- despise – look down on (someone, etc.) as inferior, worthless, or contemptible.

- diabolical – inhumanely cruel, or wicked.

- diffuse – spread out over a wide area, not concentrated.

- duo – a pair of actors, entertainers, etc.

- elaborate – detailed and complicated in design and planning.

- embassy – a residence, or offices of an ambassador.

- embossed – carve, or mould a design on a surface, so that it stands out as a relief.

- expansion – the action of becoming larger, or more extensive.

- exploits – bold, or daring feats.

- fabricate – construct, or manufacture, especially from prepared components.

- facade – outer appearance, especially a deceptive one.

- feminine – of, or characteristic of women.

- fruitlessly – useless, or unsuccessful.

- fungicidal – of the nature of, acting as, or characteristic of a fungus-destroying substance.

- gesture – an action to evoke a response, or convey intention, usually friendly.

- gourmet – food of very high quality, suitable to refined tastes.

- hangar – building with extensive floor area.

- harbour – give shelter to (especially a criminal, or wanted person).

- hatch – a door in a spacecraft.

- holographic – use, or production of holograms, a three-dimensional image formed by the interference of light beams from a laser, or other coherent light source.

- hostile – aggressively opposed; showing strong rejection.

- illuminate – light up, make bright.

- indicate – point out; make known; show.

- infamy – the state of being well known for something bad, or evil.

- intricate – very complicated, perplexingly detailed.

- invasion – an entry of a hostile army, or territory.

- listening post – a station for intercepting electronic communications.

- manoeuvre – an often deceptive planned, or controlled action, designed to gain an objective.

- marriage – a legal union between two people.

- matter printer – outputs materials from designs, loaded with unprocessed material.

- misguided – mistaken in thought, or action.

- monorail – a railway, in which, the track consists of a single rail.

- moon – natural satellite of any planet.

- mute – silent, refraining from, or temporarily incapable of speech.

- mutual – held in common, or shared by two, or more persons.

- navigate – manage, or direct the course of (ship, starcraft, etc.).

- neutrality – not helping, or supporting, either of two opposing sides.

- newlywed – a recently married person.

- nurture – foster the development of; encourage.

- observatory – a room, or building, equipped for the observation of natural (especially astronomical, or meteorological, phenomena).

- orbit – one complete passage around an orbited body.

- orientated – having a specified emphasis, bias, or interest.

- oxygen generator – device that produces O2 from power & water.

- penetrate – find access, or through, especially forcibly.

- perfume – a scented liquid.

- police state – a totalitarian state, or country, controlled by political police supervising the citizen's activities.

- pollute – contaminate (water, air, a place, etc.) with poisonous, or harmful substances.

- portal – a doorway, or gate, etc., especially a large and elaborate one.

- press release – an official statement by government department, business, etc., for information and possible publication.

- projectile – bullet, shell, etc. fired from a gun.

- prospector – a person who searches an area for gold, minerals, etc.

- provision – preparation that is made for the future.

- pulse mortar – a device that fires a projectile, when detonated, shuts down power for machines.

- regiment – a permanent unit of an army commanded by a colonel and divided into several companies.

- renowned – famous; celebrated.

- robot/drone – a machine capable of carrying out a complex series of actions automatically.

- saboteurs – a person who sabotages.

- scheme – a systematic plan, or arrangement, for work, action, etc.

- sensor – a device giving a signal for the detection, or measurement, of a physical property to which it responds.

- soap opera – a series of sensational, or melodramatic series.

- solar panel/farm – a panel that harnesses the energy in the sun's radiation, either to generate electricity using solar cells, or to heat water.

- sovereignty – the authority of a state to govern itself, or another state.

- speculate – form a theory, or opinion, about a subject without firm evidence.

- star port/stellar port – fixed outpost near star that provides products and services.

- stranded – leave a person in a place, or in a difficult situation.

- symbiotic – a partnership, or relationship, that benefits both people, or groups.

- tactic – plan, or method, used to achieve something, especially against an opponent.

- technocrat – an expert in science, technology, engineering, etc. having political power.

- teeming – present in large numbers; full of people, animals, etc. that are moving around.

- telepathically – able to communicate, or perceive thoughts, or ideas, without using speech, or writing, of any of the known senses.

- terrain – ground, a tract of land, especially with regard to its physical characteristics, or their capacity for their use by a military tactician, traveller, etc.

- trajectory – the path of an object that has been fired, launched, thrown, or hit into the air.

- tripod – a three-legged stand.

- universal translator – translates most languages and replies in the desired speech.

- vlummm – living, moving, colourful vegetation that is adored by Schlokans.

- water extractor – absorbs moisture from the land, filters it and collects it for later use.

- wedding – a marriage ceremony (considered by itself, or with associated celebrations).

- wind turbine/wind farm – a generator driven by the action of the wind on its rotating sails, or blades.

REFERENCE

Student's Oxford Canadian Dictionary, 2nd ed. Don Mills: Student's Oxford Canadian Dictionary, 2007.

ACKNOWLEDGEMENTS

This book is dedicated to my beloved daughter Riley and my sweetheart Naccole David, who has been my cheerleader from the start.

In memory of my brothers and sister:

Marty, Brent & Nicole Keryluke. Rest in peace.

CPSIA information can be obtained
at www.ICGtesting.com
Printed in the USA
LVHW070008030320
648724LV00013B/456

9 781525 546341